MAGGIE

A Sheep Dog

MAGGIE

A Sheep Dog

Dorothy Hinshaw Patent

Photographs by William Muñoz

DODD, MEAD & COMPANY

New York

Acknowledgments

The author and photographer wish to thank Richard and Shelley
Knight, J. Henry and Erma Badt, Dr. and Mrs. Henry Nichols,
and Terry and Marsha Hamilton for their help during this project
and for letting us photograph their dogs.

1 2 3 4 5 6 7 8 9 10

Library of Congress Cataloging-in-Publication Data

Patent, Dorothy Hinshaw.
   Maggie, a sheep dog.

   Summary: Follows Maggie, a type of Hungarian sheep dog known
as a Kuvasz, as she protects her sheep, runs with the flock, and
greets new baby lambs in the spring.
   1. Sheep dogs—Juvenile literature. 2. Kuvasz—Juvenile literature. [1. Kuvasz. 2. Sheep dogs]
I. Muñoz, William, ill.   II. Title.
SF428.6.P38   1986   636.7'3   85-20562
ISBN 0-396-08617-9

For Richard and Shelley Knight

MAGGIE

A Sheep Dog

Maggie is a very special dog. She has an important job. She protects sheep from danger.

Maggie is a Kuvasz (ku-vas), a kind of dog from Hungary used to guard sheep. A Kuvasz is big. It can weigh over a hundred pounds.

Training guard dogs begins when they are puppies. Their work comes naturally to them.

The puppy is left in the pasture with the sheep. It becomes attached to the sheep and they learn to trust it. As it grows older, the puppy watches over the sheep.

Maggie lives in Montana with her
owners, Richard and Shelley Knight, and
their other dog, Tootsie.

Maggie keeps an eye out for stray dogs
and coyotes that might attack her sheep.

On hot summer days, the coyotes stay in their dens. Then Maggie can lie in a cool, protected area behind the garage. Sometimes while she is resting there, Tootsie tries to get her to play.

But most of the time, Maggie lives with her sheep, summer and winter.

When the sheep are brought into a corral near the house for the night, Maggie stays with them.

Guarding sheep can sometimes get boring.

At dawn, she is with her sheep.

When the sheep are let out into the pasture in the morning, Maggie first checks the nearby woods to make sure they are safe for the sheep.

When they are moved from one pasture
to another, Maggie runs along.

When Richard must pick up a sheep to look it over, Maggie gets upset. She doesn't want anyone to hurt her sheep, even by accident.

In the afternoon, feeding time for the older sheep comes. The lambs run and jump, while their mothers mill around, waiting to be fed.

Maggie gets excited, too, and jumps into the feed trough. She is right in the middle of things, as close to her woolly friends as possible.

The sheep trust Maggie and even seem
to enjoy her company.

She shows her friendship by lying near
them and by licking them.

Maggie's brother, Ralph, also works as a guard dog. His home is on the Badt farm.

For both Maggie and Ralph, spring is
the most important time of the year. That is
when the new lambs are born.

Coyotes are especially likely to attack
then, for the lambs are not as big, strong,
and fast as their mothers.

Maggie and Ralph both stay close to the lambs to protect them.

Ralph paces back and forth, checking on the lambs.

Like the adult sheep, the lambs trust
their guardians.

The hardest time of the year for Maggie is in the fall, when the lambs are sold. Early in the morning, before the sun rises, she is lying near them.

The Knights round up the lambs and guide them into a truck. Maggie waits anxiously nearby.

Before Richard drives off with the truck, Maggie stays close to it. She doesn't want her young friends to be taken away.

As the truck rolls down the driveway,
Maggie watches it go, wanting to follow.

She tries, accompanied by Tootsie, but they cannot keep up as the truck disappears down the road.

Soon, Maggie realizes that the lambs are gone for good.

She returns to the pasture to take care of
the mother sheep.

Next spring, there will be a new crop of lambs for her to watch over.

ק.00/9.95